Meet the Original Hero on Guitar

The Galaxy's Only Rocket Star

CONTENTS

WITHDRAWN

Real Heroes Read!

realheroesread.com

#7: Guitar Rocket Star

David Anthony
and
Charles David

Illustrations
Lys Blakeslee

Traverse City, MI

Home of the Heroes

abigail

andrew

zoë

CHAPTER 1:
MEET THE HEROES

Welcome to Traverse City, Michigan, population 18,000. The city has everything you might expect: malls, movie theaters, schools, and playgrounds. Kids swim here in the summer and build snowmen during the winter. Sometimes they pretend that they live in an ordinary place.

But Traverse City is far from ordinary. It is set on one of the Great Lakes and attracts tourists in every season. Thousands of people visit every year.

Still, few of them know the city's real secret. Even fewer talk about it. You see, Traverse City is home to three gifted superheroes. This story is about them.

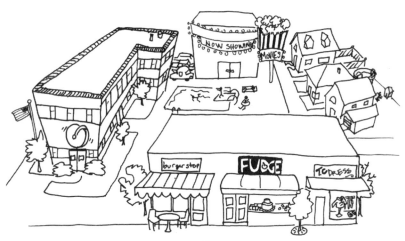

Meet Abigail, the oldest of our heroes by a whole eight minutes. When it comes to sports, she can't be beat—not at golf, not at gymnastics, and certainly not at goaltending. In fact, she's so accustomed to winning that she has become an expert at playing "We Are the Champions" on her guitar.

Andrew comes next. He's Abigail's twin brother, younger by a measly eight minutes. If it has wheels, Andrew can ride it. He's glorious, graceful, and great on wheels. He can even keep a groove while zooming downhill on his family's grand piano.

Last but definitely not least is Baby Zoë. She's proof that big things can come in small packages. She still wears a diaper, but she can flatten the strongest drum set without even trying. Zoë puts the *grrr* in *girl*.

Together these three heroes keep the streets and neighborhoods of Traverse City, Michigan, and America safe. Together they are …

CHAPTER 2:
ALARM CLOCK ROCK

Poke, poke, poke. Zoë poked her sleeping sister in the shoulder.

"Greetings," she said cheerily.

Abigail didn't stir and Zoë frowned. She was going to have to use more force, which she was good at. She sucked in a huge breath and then:

"G-O-A-L!" she shouted like an excited soccer announcer after the game-winning score.

Abigail sat straight up, and her eyes popped open. "Did we win?" she blinked sleepily. Sports always got her attention.

Zoë tried hard not to laugh. Abigail's hair was sticking up in more directions than an octopus's arms after being thrown onto the ice of Joe Louis Arena. Abigail didn't wear number 19 for nothing. Go Red Wings!

To keep quiet, Zoë quickly touched a finger to her lips. With her other hand, she pointed at Abigail's electric guitar.

"Gag," she whispered to her sister with a wink. Zoë had a plan for waking their brother. A LOUD plan.

Today was the day for loud. It was the yearly Battle of the Bands on the Bay, also called B3. In this fun competition between music groups and singers to see who was best, everyone performed and then the crowd voted by cheering.

For three years in a row, a band named Mo and the Hair Hawks had won. The band looked like real rockstars. Their leader even had a Mohawk haircut.

Nevertheless, the heroes hoped to win this year. In between saving the world and doing their homework, they had been practicing hard. In fact, sometimes they practiced *while* doing homework and saving the world. A superhero's work is never done!

This morning, however, Abigail and Zoë's work was easy. Wake up Andrew with a smile. Their smiles, that is, not his. Because they would be the ones laughing.

The girls sneaked silently out of the room. They crept quietly down the hall. And then they slinked soundlessly into Andrew's room and right up to his bed.

After that the morning was all noise. Abigail planted her feet, stood up straight, and raised her right arm into the air. A guitar pick twinkled briefly in her hand.

"Stand back," she warned Zoë. Then she brought her arm down and played an ear-splitting power-chord on her guitar.

E5!

For once Andrew didn't roll out of bed. He screamed before his wheels could even get turning.

"What's the big idea?" he gasped.

Abigail just shrugged. "Time for B3," she said sweetly.

Little did any of them know that the battle of the bands would turn into a war.

CHAPTER 3:
CHAMPIONS AT BREAKFAST

"Breakfast is ready!" Mom shouted from downstairs.

Her call interrupted the heroes, and they forgot everything but food. Mom had promised them a special meal before B3. They wondered what it could be.

"Food!" Abigail dribbled.

"Chow!" Andrew drooled.

"Grub!" Zoë slobbered, wiping her chin with her shirt.

Suddenly the three felt as if they had never been so hungry.

The meal was everything they could have hoped for. Perfect and unique for each of the heroes. When Mom prepared it, she definitely had her kids' superpowers in mind.

For Abigail, Mom served up a heaping bowl of vitamin-enriched Sporty-O's. This wasn't just a breakfast for champions. It was cereal for superheroes.

To prove it, Abigail's picture was even on the box. Thank you, Battle Creek, Michigan, where so many cereals are made.

Andrew's breakfast was a delicious combination of everything round. Mom laid it out before him like a Thanksgiving feast. All he needed to do was catch it with his fork before it rolled away.

Of course he still had time to play. He snatched the halves of a buttery bagel and held them up to his eyes.

"I'm Bagel Boy," he said in a phony deep voice. "Tell me the *hole* truth and nothing but the *hole* truth."

Zoë crossed her eyes. "Goober," she muttered.

Zoë didn't need a fancy breakfast. She ate the same thing she ate every morning—S.U.P.E.R. Baby Formula. S.U.P.E.R. stood for Secret Ultra-Potent Enhancement Recipe. Mom suspected it gave Zoë her superpowers. Zoë just liked the taste.

"Growing," she said between mouthfuls. Her muscles really did feel enhanced!

Cleaning up after breakfast was almost as fun as eating. Why? Because superpowers could be used for good, but also for good times.

Plates, bowls, cups, and saucers all have one thing in common. They are round. So Andrew wheeled them into the dishwasher like a bowler on the pro tour.

"Slam dunk!" Abigail cheered, flipping the dishwasher's door closed.

The heroes' work was done. It was time to go to the Battle of the Bands on the Bay.

CHAPTER 4:
TOUR TRAIN

"I have a surprise for you," Andrew told his sisters. "Go wait for me in the driveway." Then he vanished out the side door and into the garage.

Abigail and Zoë shared an alarmed look. "He's up to something," Abigail said. "We'd better hurry before he hurts himself."

"Grrreeeaaat," Zoë sighed, rolling her eyes.

The girls knew from experience that Andrew's surprises usually meant danger. Fast danger. Their brother could and would do anything with a wheel.

Correction. Make that sixteen wheels. Andrew had outdone himself this time. His latest speedy surprise was more than a four-by-four. It was a four times four equals sixteen wheels.

"What do you think?" Andrew grinned from the driver's seat. "If we want to play like rock stars, then we have to travel like rock stars."

Andrew had hitched three wagons to his four-wheeler and packed them with musical instruments, amplifiers, and speakers. Some rock stars rode a on a tour bus. Today the heroes would be cruising on a tour train.

Best of all, Andrew didn't scare his sisters with his antics behind the wheel. He kept to the right, kept his eyes on the road, and kept his speed down.

Abigail smiled to herself. "Keep it up," she snickered.

Officer Duncan McDonought appreciated Andrew's driving, too. He gave the hero a thumb's-up when Andrew pulled into the B3 parking lot. That was better than the usual traffic ticket.

The beach was packed. People stood shoulder to shoulder on the sand. Some waded in the water. One strange figure was even collecting stones in a bucket.

Nowhere, however, was busier than the autograph table. Frenzied fans formed a back-and-forth line in front of the table as if waiting to ride a roller coaster. The lead singer of Mo and the Hair Hawks was signing autographs!

Mo spotted the heroes and looked up with a smirk on his face.

"Hey, Andrew and Abigail," he called. "Did that baby learn to play yet?"

By baby, he meant Zoë. She had been too young to play the real drums at last year's B3. So she had played the one instrument that all babies could play. The rattle.

Not a big hit with the fans.

"Grrr," Zoë growled, getting ready to tell Mo to hush. She had quit playing with rattles weeks ago!

Lucky for him, an obnoxious voice cut her off. It boomed over the P.A. system like a commercial that was twice as loud as the show.

"Yo, yo, yo," blared M.C. Blabber, the cheesy disc jockey. "Let's get this battle started!"

After he spoke, the crowd cheered and the heroes gulped. The Battle of the Bands on the Bay was about to begin.

CHAPTER 5:
B3

"First up today is Traverse City's singing sweetheart," M.C. Blabber shouted into his microphone. "She likes kissing frogs, long carriage rides, and dancing in glass slippers. Give it up for Little Princess!"

The crowd cheered again, and the heroes tried not to grin. Little Princess was their neighbor, but today she had transformed herself into a hip-hop star.

My name is Little Princess.
You can check my crown.
I'm the hippest royal rapper
In this T.C. town.

When Little Princess finished her song, M.C. Blabber introduced the next performer.

"All right, dudes and dudettes, it's time to hold onto your carrots. Our next musician's teeth have a beef with everything orange. Let's hear it for Rappin' Rabbit!"

A pounding drumbeat shook the ground as Rappin' Rabbit took the stage. He was Little Princess's big brother, but you couldn't tell by look-ing at them. Rappin' Rabbit resembled the Easter Bunny more than his sister.

Give it up for the bunny.
Give it up for the hare.
Give it up for the Rabbit.
Put your ears in the air.

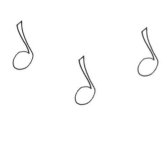

   A variety of groups followed Rappin' Rabbit,
including some unusual newcomers. Freddie Fudge
fired up the fans, the Mackinaw Maniacs maddened
the masses, and Cherie and the Blossoms blew away
the bay. Their unique music could be heard as far
away as Waunakee, Wisconsin.

Finally the heroes' turn came. Their round to rock had arrived.

"The next group needs little introduction," the disc jockey announced. "You may know them as Abigail, Andrew, and Zoë. Or you may know their super identities—Triple-A, Kid Roll, and Zuper Zoë. Either way, let's cheer it up for Heroes A^{2}Z!"

Zoë swooped onto stage and plopped down behind her drum set. She twirled drumsticks over her head in both hands. Then she whacked them together three times and shouted, "Go, go, go!"

Fingers flying on her guitar, Abigail slid into view on her knees. Baseball players like her didn't usually slide into first base, but Abigail had a different first in mind. Today she was aiming for first place in the Battle of the Bands on the Bay.

Andrew shared her goal but had his own style. He wheeled onto stage riding a bicycle built for two. Two-plus-86 keys, that is. Piano keys.

He could and would do anything with a wheel, remember? Leave it to Andrew to give a whole new meaning to rock-n-roll!

Just as the heroes were about to start singing, an explosion burst overhead.

BOOM!

The noise caused Zoë to drop her drumsticks. Abigail broke a string, and Andrew hit such a bad note that every dog in Traverse City started to howl.

Worst of all, the boom was followed by a flash of light and fire in the sky.

"Gadzooks!" Zoë exclaimed, squinting upward.

It looked as if a blazing comet was going to crash right onto the stage.

CHAPTER 6:
BENJAMIN AXE

"Look out!" someone in the audience shouted.

"It's coming right at us!" cried another.

The comet was racing rapidly closer. Fire and smoke churned in its wake. High-pitched squeals wailed on the wind like an off-key guitar solo.

In fact, the comet didn't just sound like a guitar. It looked like a guitar. A giant metal guitar with wings and rocket boosters.

No one in the audience shouted the usual "It's a bird!" or "It's a plane!" as the strange flying object came in for a landing on stage. Zoë summed up everyone's thoughts with just one word.

"Guitar," she said, pointing.

The comet wasn't a comet. It was a rocket from outer space. Words were printed on its side like a billboard.

For long moments, everything and everyone went silent. The crowd held its breath. The rocket stopped squealing. Not a soul made a peep on the beach.

Finally M.C. Blabber cleared his throat and spoke falteringly into his microphone.

"*I*-I'm being told that we *h*-have a new contestant," he stammered, tapping his headset. Instructions were being spoken into his earphones. "Please help me welcome the one and only Guitar Rocket Star—Benjamin Axe and his Mullet Mob!"

Chunk!

A heavy sound clanked inside the rocket, and then jets of steam spurted from vents along its surface. Slowly a tall door lowered like a castle drawbridge.

Now the crowd breathed again. They exhaled long enough to gasp. Something was coming out of the rocket. But what?

The something coming out of the rocket wasn't alone. A dozen somethings or more tumbled out of the door before it was even halfway open.

The somethings looked like walking hairballs. They were about the size of gallon milk jugs and had flat bare feet. Nothing else could be seen of them because of all the hair. It was shaggy on all sides but extra long in back.

"It's the Mullet Mob!" the heroes' Dad shouted. "They look like mullet haircuts with feet."

The mullet had been a very popular hairstyle during the early 1990s. It was short hair in the front, long in back. Miley Cyrus's dad had worn one of the most famous mullets of all.

The rocket's door landed gently on the ground, and the steam slowly cleared. As it did, a proud shape took its place.

It was a tall, thin man holding a triangular guitar. He confidently raised one finger into the air.

"I am Benjamin Axe," he declared in a high voice. "I am here to rock your world!"

CHAPTER 7:
THE WORLD IS MINE

"Do you want to hear some rock?" Benjamin Axe howled into the crowd. "Do you want to hear some roll?" His high voice hit even higher notes on the words *rock* and *roll.*

Cheering, the crowd rushed forward. They jammed themselves up against the stage and began chanting. "Rock! Rock! Rock!"

Benjamin Axe took their reaction as a "yes." He raised an arm above his guitar and leaned into the microphone.

"I call this song 'The World Is Mine.'"

The introduction to the song was fast, but the song was even faster. Benjamin Axe's fingers blurred over his guitar. Singing backup, the Mullet Mob stomped and twirled to the beat behind him.

> *I'm here to rock (Rock!)*
> *I'm here to roll (Roll!)*
> *I'm here to steal your mind and soul*
>
> *I'm here to play (Play!)*
> *I'm here to jam (Jam!)*
> *I'm here to deal my music scam*

A strange thing happened while Axe played. His amplifiers and speakers spat music notes into the air like snow blowers throwing snow. The notes drifted into the crowd like bubbles.

Most of the audience didn't pay attention to the notes. They were too interested in Benjamin Axe's music.

So Zoë kept a watchful eye on things. Make that two eyes. She zapped every note that came near her and her siblings.

Bzzt! Her eye lasers zapped a note floating over Abigail's head. *Bzzt!* She struck a second to the right of Andrew's ear.

Even the heroes' parents were enjoying Axe's performance. During a break between songs, Dad turned to his kids with a huge smile on his face.

"This is totally awesome, dudes," he said like a surfer. "Like the old days when I was young. Long guitar solos and longer hair. *Y-e-a-h!*"

To make his point, he wiggled his fingers, playing air guitar.

Ten songs later, Axe took a final bow.

"You've been a great crowd, Traverse City!" he half-sang and half-screeched. "Thank you and goodnight!"

He tried to close the curtain on the stage then, but the crowd wouldn't let him. They climbed onto the stage, grabbed Axe, and heaved him onto their shoulders.

"Number one!" the cheered. "Number one!"

The judges agreed. They unanimously awarded Benjamin Axe the B3 winner's trophy. The heroes weren't given time to finish their song. Mo and the Hair Hawks didn't even play.

Benjamin Axe had won the Battle of the Bands on the Bay.

48

CHAPTER 8:
MULLET MOB

Stunned. That was how the heroes felt. One moment they had been rocking on stage. Driving drums, grinding guitars, kicking keyboards. The next a spaceman had come down to steal their spotlight.

What a disappointment!

Now the Battle of the Bands on the Bay was over. The heroes had lost, and Benjamin Axe had won. Stunning.

"Gone," Zoë sighed, meaning the concert, the excitement, and the hope of winning. Say goodbye to B3. Better luck next year.

Her brother and sister were too stunned to even speak. They had lost. Heroes like them! Defeated.

So they packed their instruments in silence. They rode home in silence. And the got ready for bed in silence. A trio of mimes performing at the library made more noise.

The next morning the heroes still didn't feel much like talking. Defeated? Heroes like them? But what they saw at the breakfast table made them shout.

"Mom?" Andrew gasped.

"Dad!" exclaimed Abigail.

"Guys?" Zoë asked in alarm.

Their parents were sitting in the same spots they had been sitting in the night before. They hadn't moved. They hadn't slept. They were listening to loud rock-n-roll music blaring from headphones on their ears.

The headphones looked like music notes. Just like the ones that had floated out of the speakers at the concert last night. Just like the ones that Zoë had zapped.

"Grave!" she said, recognizing grave danger when she heard it. The music coming from the headphones was Benjamin Axe's opening song.

I'm here to rock (Rock!)
I'm here to roll (Roll!)
I'm here to steal your mind and soul.

Mom and Dad had been listening to it all night long. They were hypnotized!

Zoë reached for the headphones on Mom's ears first. She wanted to zap them and make the music stop.

When her fingers got near the headphones, something moved in Mom's hair. Something fast and with nasty teeth.

Chomp!

It darted out and bit Zoë's hand.

"A mullet!" Abigail cried. "From the Mullet Mob! It's in Mom's hair!"

As soon as she spoke, Abigail realized how wrong she was. There wasn't just one mullet in Mom's hair. There were five.

And all of them sprang out to attack at once.

CHAPTER 9:
HAIR WEAKNESS

"There's more of them!" Abigail cried.

Now she knew the truth. Five mullet monsters had leaped out of Mom's hair. Three at her and two toward her brother. Her cry was their only defense.

It failed.

The mullets snatched her and Andrew, lassoing them like cowboys from the Old West. Only these cowboys didn't hurl ropes. They swung strands of hair.

Ride 'em, hairbrush!

Down went the twins, roped like doggies. Abigail's gave a little bark, even less bite. They didn't even put up a fight.

Zoë wanted to change that. She had plenty of fight to share. Especially for monsters named after haircuts that were twenty years out of style.

Twenty years! Zoë couldn't imagine being alive that long. What had the world been like twenty years ago?

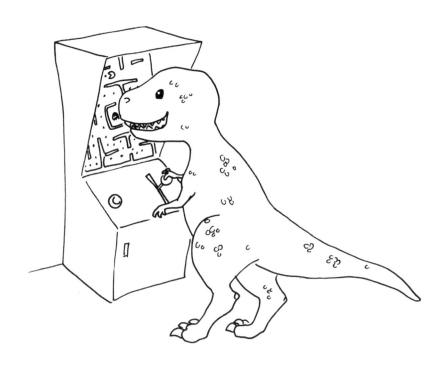

Not that now was the safest time to wonder. Zoë needed to think about the present or she would be history.

But who should she help first? Two mullets held Andrew hostage. Three had her sister snared. Five more were whirling braids over their heads like a free-for-all at the rodeo.

What! Five more? The mullets were multiplying! First five, now ten. Zoë didn't need a calculator to know that meant double trouble.

Up she sped toward the ceiling, barely ahead of the mullets. She hated running away, but she couldn't let the monsters catch her. She was the only member of her family still free.

The mullets attacked from the ground. They launched long strands of hair at her like Spider-man's webs. Most smacked and bounced against the ceiling. But one lucky shot connected with Zoë's ankle. It wrapped around her ankle and started to drag her down.

Grrr! The mullets were strong. Zoë couldn't pull away. She huffed, puffed, and acted gruff, but she quickly lost ground in the air.

What she needed was a secret weapon. Something that would break the mullet's grip. Question was, what? She considered several options.

Tickling? Too risky. Who knew what was under all that hair.

Salt? That was supposed to work on leeches. But eww, no thanks. Pass.

Shampoo? The mullets were made of hair. Could shampoo be their weakness?

Their weakness. What about hair weakness?

Suddenly Zoë had it. A simple solution. Nothing got the better of hair than a pair of good scissors. Snip, snip. Dark or light, short or long. Scissors made hair be gone.

Unless they were trying to cut Zoë's hair, that was. Scissors usually ended up in the scrap heap when they met her.

Dodging right, then spinning left, Zoë zipped to the junk drawer. It was called that because the drawer contained a little bit of everything and a lot of who-knows-what. Can't figure out what something is? Put it in the junk drawer. Someone will probably need it later.

Lucky for Zoë, the drawer also contained scissors.

"Goody!" she exclaimed, snatching the scissors and raising them above her head like a sword.

That was all it took. Scissors terrified the mullets. The creatures immediately released the heroes and fled. Good news for the heroes, bad news for Mom and Dad. Because the mullets scampered up the kitchen chairs, across the table, and back into Mom and Dad's hair.

Everything was back to the way it had been when the heroes first entered the kitchen. Mom and Dad were hypnotized, and rock-n-roll blared out of their music note-shaped headphones.

"Groovy," Mom said, sounding like Zoë.

CHAPTER 10:
GUITAR GETAWAY

"Giddy-up!" Zoë said, pointing outside.

She and her siblings couldn't help Mom and Dad by staying in the kitchen. They needed to find Benjamin Axe. His music had hypnotized their parents, and his mullets were guarding their hair. It didn't take a music instructor to realize that Axe was out of tune.

"Race you there," Andrew shouted, halfway out the door. He was way ahead of Zoë and already on the way back to the beach.

Yet even with a head start, Andrew didn't win the race. Abigail sprinted past him before he reached the edge of the yard. Zoë flew by a second later.

"Phooey on feet," Andrew grumbled. He might not be able to outrun his sisters, but he could out-roll them. So he tucked in his chin and somersaulted over the grass.

When he leaped up, he wasn't just Andrew anymore. He had sprouted wheels and changed into his not-so-secret identity. He had become Kid Roll.

"Time to burn rubber!" he cheered.

Now the race was really on. Andrew rolled,
Zoë was bold, and Abigail went all out for gold. But
truth be told, no one won. The race to the beach
ended up in a three-way tie. No winners, no losers.
Except for the hundreds of people already there. They
had lost a different race. The race to escape Benjamin Axe. All of them had been hypnotized by the
spaceman's mesmerizing music.

The heroes froze. What a sight! So many people, and all of them hypnotized. The beached looked like a wax museum filled with statues wearing headphones.

Only the disc jockey M.C. Blabber seemed to notice the heroes. He still sat in front of his microphone, but he was also wearing music note headphones.

"Attention, rockers and rollers," he said over the loudspeakers. "Michigan's so-called superheroes have finally returned. Too bad they missed the final performance. Mr. Axe has left the stage."

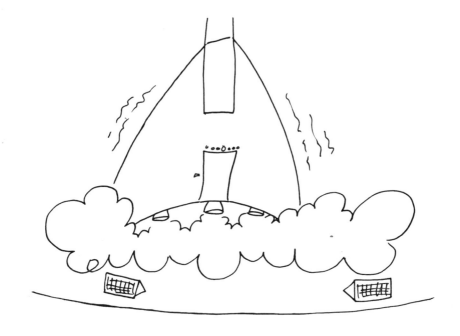

Before the heroes had time to wonder what that meant, Benjamin Axe's spaceship roared to life. Smoke belched out of its engine, and the squealing sounds of an electric guitar forced the heroes to cover their ears.

"Getaway!" Zoë cried, the first to recover.

Benjamin Axe really had left the stage, and he wasn't stopping there. After his ship took off, he could go anywhere. The heroes had to stop him now or else!

CHAPTER 11:
COUNTDOWN

"Ten," M.C. Blabber spoke slowly into his microphone. A pause as long as one-Mississippi followed. Then: "Nine," said the DJ.

"It's a countdown!" Abigail exclaimed. "For Axe's ship. It will launch when the DJ gets to zero."

"Eight."

"Zoë, throw me," Andrew said. "Like you did at the mall.* It's the only way to get past all of the people."

"Seven."

The only way? No, probably not. But it was a good way, and Zoë was glad to help. She snatched Andrew by the shoulders, lifted him over her head, and threw.

*See Heroes A2Z #5: Easter Egg Haunt

"Six."

Crash!

Zoë's throw was good, and her aim was better. Andrew soared over the crowd, across the stage, and smacked into the side of Benjamin Axe's guitar-shaped rocket.

"Gotcha!" Zoë beamed. Then she turned to her sister, ready to throw again.

"Five."

"No thanks," Abigail said quickly. "I can make it over myself."

"Four!"

To prove it, Abigail rapidly pulled a very long pole from her duffel bag. Too long, in fact, to fit in an ordinary bag. But this bag was special. It could hold all of the sports equipment Abigail would ever need and still never weigh her down. It could even hold a 12-foot pole.

"Three!"

"Watch your toes," Abigail advised.

Then she started to run while holding the pole in front of her like a knight's lance. Just before running into the hypnotized crowd, she planted the pole, jumped, and let the pole carry her into the air.

For a moment, Abigail was flying. Look out, Zoë! Watch it, Superman. Michigan had two hovering heroes now.

Up and over the crowd Abigail soared. Up, over, and onto the stage. She landed softly next to Andrew and helped him to his feet.

"Two!"

Abigail grinned at her brother. "Think Detroit Red Wings hockey," she teased. "Their logo is a winged wheel. It might help you fly next time."

Andrew just stuck out his tongue.

Zoë reached the rocket last, but just in time.
"One!"

"Grab!" she told her siblings. The rocket was about to—

"Blast off!"

Suddenly more smoke erupted from the engines, and the whole rocket started to shake. The sound of screeching guitars wailed like fireworks on the Fourth of July.

Just as the rocket leaped into the air, the heroes grabbed on. Wherever it was going, they were going, too. What a wild ride it would be.

CHAPTER 12:
HITCH A RIDE

Up, up, up. Benjamin Axe's rocket hurtled higher into the sky. The people below already looked like ants. Soon Traverse City would be just a colorful blob.

The heroes had to stop the rocket!

Zoë rapped her tiny fist on the ship's hull like a sledgehammer. Boom, boom, boom!

"Ground!" she demanded like a police officer pulling over a speeder. Today she was the law. The Law of Gravity. And she wanted Benjamin Axe to obey.

Safely inside his rocket, Benjamin Axe laughed. So the heroes wanted to hitch a ride? He would give them one they would never forget.

Whoosh!

North he sped, and east. Out over Lake Michigan and across the Mackinaw Bridge. Then down into the chilly waters of Lake Superior he plunged.

Sploosh!

Air! The heroes took one last gulp. Then they held their breath as the rocket dove deep into the icy water.

So deep, in fact, that a murky sight took shape. It was the Edmund Fitzgerald, a famous shipwreck. The ship had sunk in 1975 and inspired folk stories for decades. In fact, many songs had been written about it, including Gordon Lightfoot's haunting hit "Wreck of the Edmund Fitzgerald."

Before the heroes saw much of the famous ship, Benjamin Axe turned his rocket upward again. He wasn't taking them on a sight seeing tour. He had more dangerous plans.

Seconds later, the rocket burst from the water, and an explanation burst from Zoë's lips.

"G-force!" she shouted, and the twins agreed. Benjamin Axe was trying to knock them off his rocket like a bucking bronco at the rodeo.

To do so, he sped north and south, east and west. He drilled his way down oil fields near Midland.

He burrowed through the Detroit-Windsor Tunnel to Canada.

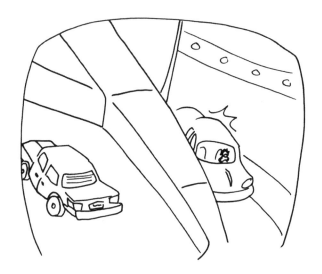

He wandered the maze of tall buildings in Grand Rapids.

And he hiked up the heights of the Porcupine Mountains.

Finally Axe was willing to give up. He had tried shaking, rattling, and rolling. Nothing worked. The heroes were still on the charts.

"You kids sure know how to rock and roll," he said over the rocket's intercom. "How about joining my band?"

Zoë answered for everyone right away. "Gross!" In other words, no thanks and no way.

Benjamin Axe shook his head. "I was afraid you would say that. So goodbye, heroes. You shooting stars are about to become has-beens."

With that, he jammed his rocket into overdrive. Next stop: outer space.

CHAPTER 13:
FROZEN FALL

Benjamin Axe's rocket climbed higher and higher. Soon the ground vanished beneath the clouds, and the air turned bitter cold.

"I'm *f*-freezing," Andrew shivered.

Clinging to the side of the rocket, he and his sisters were quickly turning into human snowmen. Ice covered them from head to toe like morning frost.

"*C*-can't h-hold on," Abigail stuttered, teeth chattering. "I'm out!"

The cold was too much. Her fingers stiffened and slipped. She fell.

"Abigail!" Andrew shrieked. He wildly swiped an arm after her but missed. Strike! Then he lost his grip and fell, too. Another out.

A moment later Zoë made it three up and three down. She couldn't let his siblings fall alone. So she took a deep breath and let go.

Normally falling wasn't dangerous to her. Zoë could fly. She could even fly and carry her siblings at the same time. Not that Andrew and Abigail allowed it often. They preferred to depend on their own superpowers, not Zoë's.

But today Zoë couldn't fly. Today she was covered in ice and falling. Today was dangerous.

She dropped out of the sky as if wearing a suit of armor and holding buckets filled with Petoskey stones* in her hands.

"Gerinomo!" she wailed.

*See Heroes A2Z #4: Digging for Dinos

B-O-O-O-O-M!

Zoë landed first, crashing into the Porcupine Mountains like a meteorite. Into was the right word, too, because she didn't just hit the ground and stop. She struck it so hard that she caused a crater like those on the moon.

The ice covering Zoë kept her safe, but it also shattered on impact. She was free, and just in time.

Right hand catch! She grabbed Abigail.

Left hand snatch! She caught Andrew.

The heroes gasped for air. What a landing! They should have been flattened. Sometimes they escaped danger with their skill and strength. Sometimes they just got lucky.

"Everyone okay?" Abigail asked. She was already up and digging through her duffel bag for rock climbing gear. The All-American Athlete would get her siblings out of this crater.

"I'm fine," Andrew responded.

"Good," Zoë said, but she quickly changed her mind.

A huge shadow swept over the mountains, the crater, and then the heroes. It was cast by Benjamin Axe's ship. The guitar rocket star wasn't finished with them yet.

CHAPTER 14:
NOTEWORTHY PRISON

"Gloomy," Zoë whispered, gazing up at Benjamin Axe's rocket.

The spacecraft draped a deep shadow over the heroes. They were trapped beneath it in the crater. There was gloom above and gloom all around. No escape.

"This was your final performance," Benjamin Axe said over the loudspeakers. "Goodnight!"

Like an exclamation point, the sound of more squealing guitar followed his words. It screeched again and again like the revving of a motorcycle's engine.

And with every shriek, the rocket fired a musical missile toward the heroes.

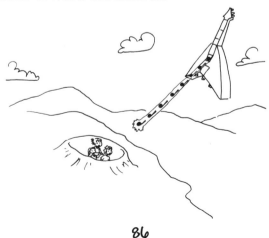

Missile after missile rocked from Axe's rocket. Sixteen shots on sixteen beats in standard time and rhythm.

When their noise finally faded, the missiles didn't explode. They didn't strike and erupt. Instead they became solid like water that had turned into ice. They lay across the crater's opening in lines like the bars of a prison cell.

Andrew stared up at the bars and laughed. "You've got a flat tire, Axe!" he teased. "Zoë has broken out of jail before."*

Abigail nodded and grinned at her little sister. "Batter up, Zoë. Show Benjamin Axe that prison is for villains, not superheroes."

"Gladly," Zoë said, floating upward and cracking her knuckles. But when she grasped the bars overhead, she was forced to let go.

*See Heroes A2Z #7: Fowl Mouthwash

The noise!

As soon as her fingers touched the bars, a guitar squealed louder than she had ever heard before.

Her hands immediately went to her ears, but the damage was done. Zoë stumbled in midair, spinning dizzily. Her head throbbed and her ears rang. She was flying out of control.

This was why parents told their kids to turn the music down.

Thinking fast, Andrew jumped, rolled, and caught Zoë before she crashed. The tiny hero was still dazed.

"We'll find another way out of here!" Abigail shouted at Benjamin Axe. Once again, she was already digging through her duffel bag for something that would help her and her siblings escape.

"I'm counting on it," Benjamin Axe replied, not the least bit afraid. "My encore will rock your socks off. See you in Ohio!"

With that, he turned his rocket around and punched the accelerator. *Whooosh!* A moment later he and his ship were gone.

CHAPTER 15:
OFF TO OHIO

Ohio? Why was Benjamin Axe going to Ohio? That was the question on all three of the heroes' minds.

Sure, they knew that Ohio was the state directly south of Michigan. They also knew its capital was Columbus. But those facts didn't explain why Benjamin Axe was going there.

"Maybe he wants to visit Cedar Point?" Andrew suggested. Cedar Point was an amusement park with roller coasters, log rides, bumper cars, and lots more. It was awesome fun.

Now it was Abigail's turn to shake her head. The answer seemed so obvious to her. There was one place in Ohio to see before all others.

"The pro football Hall of Fame," she said confidently. No question about it.

At least not until Andrew snapped his fingers and spoke.

"That's it, Abigail!" he exclaimed. "Well, sort of. Axe is going to the Hall of Fame, all right. The *Rock and Roll* Hall of Fame."

His sisters instantly agreed. The Rock and Roll Hall of Fame in Cleveland, Ohio was where they needed to be.

"Gate," Zoë muttered, glancing at the bars above. For once, her flying power and strength were useless.

"Don't worry," Abigail smirked as if she had a secret. "I'll get us out before the final buzzer."

She immediately started to dig a tunnel with her sporting equipment. She hacked with hockey sticks, bashed with baseball bats, and pulverized with polo mallets. Almost nothing in her duffel bag went unused.

She didn't stop until she reached Ohio either. That was her personal finish line. Anything less, and she wouldn't be giving 100%.

Besides, Andrew could roll all the way to Ohio. Zoë could fly there in a flash. Did you doubt the All-American Athlete could travel as fast and far? Shame on you!

When Abigail finally lowered her mallet, the dust settled slowly. Light shone down from a man-hole cover above.

"*Wh*-who wants to peek first?" she panted.

Zoë zipped into action. Lifting the manhole cover and scooting it aside was simple. Keeping herself from gasping at what she saw beyond it was not.

Stapled to a telephone pole was an old-fashioned black-and-white wanted poster. It looked like something out of the Old West.

Three hand-drawn faces scowled at Zoë with dark eyes. The poster named them Abominable Abigail, Awful Andrew, and Zoë the Zero.

The heroes were wanted like criminals! The reward? Free headphones. Oh, sure! Like Benjamin Axe wasn't already giving those away.

CHAPTER 16:
HAIR FORCE ONE

Cleveland, Ohio didn't look too much different from Traverse City. Sure it was bigger and had more tall buildings, but today the danger was the same.

Hypnotized people filled the streets and sidewalks. All of them wore music note-shaped headphones. All of them had mullets in their hair.

Had Benjamin Axe hypnotized the whole world already?

"Put it in gear," Andrew whispered. "We have to move."

Being in the streets with all the mullets nearby was like swimming in the open ocean. Sharks were everywhere and could strike at any time.

As calmly as they could, the heroes climbed out of the manhole. They picked a direction and started walking. No sudden movements. No loud noises. Just three kids taking a stroll.

Still, by the time they had gone two blocks, they had attracted too much attention. A herd of mangy mullets followed closely behind them.

"In here," Abigail said, pointing at a storefront. It belonged to a beauty salon named Hair Force One. Its logo was a jet airplane wearing a long curly wig.

Andrew balked. "I'm not going in there. That place is for girls."

His sisters didn't argue. They just pushed him through the door.

"Geek," Zoë snickered.

Once the heroes were inside the salon, Abigail started giving orders. She was a head coach, team captain, and cheerleader all rolled into one package.

"Zoë, play cowboy," she said. "The hairdryers can be your six-shooters."

When she turned to Andrew, he raised his arms defensively.

"Oh, no," he protested. "No way. I am not going to be her faithful companion." By faithful companion, he meant horse. Every cowboy was supposed to have one.

Abigail smirked. "Maybe later," she winked. "Right now, find something round. Maybe some curlers. They'll roll. You should like that."

As for herself, Abigail found plenty of what she wanted. She scooped up bottle after bottle of her secret weapon. When she couldn't carry any more, she said, "Open the door."

It was time to take care of the mullets.

CHAPTER 17:
SALON TREATMENT

It didn't take the Abigail, Andrew, and Zoë long to find the mullets. In fact, the mullets were waiting for them outside. The hairy little brutes were everywhere—in the street, on the sidewalk, and crawling over cars.

Cleveland was completely overrun!

"Andrew, you're batting lead-off," Abigail said as she flung open the door to Hair Force One. Show them what you've got!"

Andrew rolled instantly into action. He somersaulted out the door and sprang to his feet. All the while, he tossed hair curlers at the mullets.

After that, it was all curlers. Andrew didn't have to do another thing. The curlers rolled over the sidewalk, onto the pavement, and into the nearest pack of mullets. Not even sporty Abigail could have bowled a more perfect strike.

Vroo-oop! Vroop-vroop!

When the curlers and mullets collided, the curlers won every time. They snagged the mullets, wouldn't let go, and rolled them up like blinds in a window.

"Gust!" Zoë cheered, swooping into action next. Andrew had eliminated the first mob of mullets. It was her job to take care of the second.

Armed with a hairdryer in each hand, Zoë charged fearlessly into battle. Zap! She fired over her shoulder. Zap! She shot between her legs.

Mullets everywhere tumbled and twirled through the air. They couldn't stand up to two hairdryers. No hair could take the heat! Zoë's double barrels blew them away like wisps on the wind.

So far away that Abigail had the time she needed to stop the mullets for good. Or, she hoped, at least for a good long time. She and her siblings needed to stop Benjamin Axe, not only his hairy hoodlums.

Squick! Squick! Squick!

She quickly cranked the button on the top of her first bottle. Liquid blasted from its nozzle and soaked the closest mullet. The fuzzy creature blinked once and then froze. It couldn't move. It was stuck and Abigail grinned. Her secret weapon worked. Hairspray stopped the mullets like a futuristic freeze ray.

Her grin, however, didn't last long. The sound of a familiar high-pitched voice vanquished it from her face.

"So you're back for an encore?" said Benjamin Axe.

Abigail spun to see the guitar rocket star floating in the air above her. He glared down at her from a hoverboard that was shaped like a guitar.

"What a shame for you," he continued. "That I get to pick the last song. I call it 'Heavy Metal Hydra.'"

Then he raised his arm and swiftly brought it down. His guitar erupted with thunderous noise.

CHAPTER 18:
HEAVY METAL HYDRA

Benjamin Axe wailed on his guitar, took aim, and fired. *Floom!* A bolt of furious sound burst from his instrument like a shot from a laser canon.

The heroes scattered, running, rolling, and racing in different directions. But that wasn't necessary. Axe's noisy shot wasn't meant for them. Benjamin Axe had fired at the building behind them. The building was the Rock and Roll Hall of Fame. The Rock Hall. The heroes had found it without searching. They had wandered right up to it during their battle with the mullets.

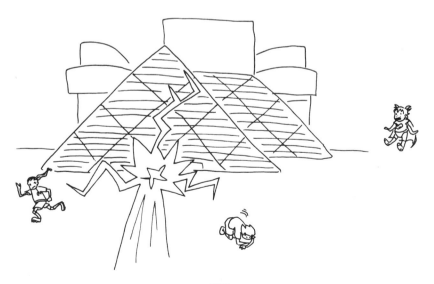

Unfortunately the heroes got only a brief glance at the majestic museum. Benjamin Axe's attack struck immediately.

Ka-Boooom!

The Hall of Fame exploded. Glass shattered, shrieking, and metal twisted, screeching. Smoke and dust rose in a thick black cloud. The sound of heavy drumbeats rumbled within it.

"Gargantuan!" Zoë gasped, the first to spot something in the cloud.

As the dust and smoke settled, a huge shape appeared. It was a monster out of legend—a dragon with three heads on three long necks. It was also at least thirty feet tall.

"A hydra," Andrew whispered. He had read stories about such monsters, but hydras weren't supposed to live in Ohio. They weren't even supposed to be real!

But this hydra was all kinds of real. Real big, real angry, and real loud. When it opened its mouths and showed its teeth, the heroes scattered again.

Though again it did them no good. The hydra didn't bite and it didn't breathe fire. It didn't even need to touch the heroes to defeat them.

Instead it sucked in three huge gulps of air and started to sing.

Yes, sing. The hydra sang three different songs from its three different mouths.

The left head sang a lullaby. Sweet, soft words drifted peacefully to Abigail's ears. She tried to ignore them but failed. After sprinting less than ten feet, she fell soundly asleep like a well-fed baby in a crib.

Andrew heard the blues. The hyrdra's middle head sang to him. Lyrics of loss and woe wrenched his heart. A lost dog. A best friend moved away. A flat tire on a brand new bike. How sad!

Finally he couldn't take anymore. He flopped down on the curb with his head in his hands. He was too depressed to go on.

The right and last head sang to Zoë. Unlike the others, its song was loud and full of force. Bolts like lightning spat from its mouth.

Zoë yelped and zigzagged through the air. Howling bolts streaked all around her. They shattered buildings, cars, buses, and concrete. Imagine what they would do to a baby in a diaper!

Dodging this way and that, she quickly scooped up her siblings and fled. Benjamin Axe had won this battle, but Zoë promised to return.

CHAPTER 19:
PREHISTORIC PRETZEL

After Zoë had them far enough away from the hydra, Abigail and Andrew came to their senses.

"No wonder Axe picked Cleveland," Andrew said. "He made his monster from the Rock and Roll Hall of Fame. Just think of all that musical muscle!"

His sisters nodded. "But what's the hydra's weakness?" Abigail wondered. "Even Superman has kryptonite. The hydra must have a weakness, too."

Zoë shrugged and said the first thing that came to mind. "Gibson."

She had noticed Benjamin Axe controlling the hydra with his Gibson guitar the whole time. Gibson was a famous brand of guitars.

Once again, Zoë had done it. With just one word, she had given the heroes a plan.

"Okay," Abigail said to her sister. "You take out Axe. Andrew and I will distract the hydra."

Andrew blinked. "We will? How?"

He hoped for something big and heavy, like gaint barbells or a football team. What Abigail showed him was slightly smaller.

"Earplugs," she announced. She held up a tiny pair of swimmer's earplugs and smiled like an actor in a gum commercial.

Neither Zoë nor Andrew had a better plan, so they just looked at one another and shrugged. Earplugs. Why not? They were small but that didn't mean useless. Zoë was small but she could save the world but still be home before dinner. Elephants were supposedly frightened by mice.

Earplugs might be exactly what the heroes needed to defeat the hydra.

Earplugs and a whole lot of superpower, that is.

Abigail led the charge. She wore earplugs in her ears and clutched a baseball bat and ball in her hands. When the hydra started to sing, she didn't hear a note. She tossed her ball into the air and swung. Crack!

"It's outta here," Abigail cheered. A hydra homerun.

The ball soared over the hydra's middle head. Back, back, back it went, and so did the head.

"Now!" Abigail shouted to her brother. "Go!"

She tore off to the right like a baseball all-star running the bases. Andrew spun left, rolling the opposite way.

The hydra tried to follow them both. One head went right, one went left, and the last turned round and round.

"Check out the prehistoric pretzel!" Andrew whooped. The hydra might not be a dinosaur, but it was definitely tying itself in knots.

Not that knots were enough for Zoë. She wouldn't let the battle end in a tie. Like Abigail earlier, Zoë had a secret weapon.

"Graceland!" she cried, calling on the one musical force that was stronger than the Hall of Fame.

She called upon Elvis Presley, the King of Rock and Roll. Graceland had been his home. It would take the electric power of Elvis Presley to defeat the bad attitude of Benjamin Axe.

CHAPTER 20:
GIVING BEN THE AXE

From the rubble of the Rock and Roll Hall of Fame, Zoë pulled an Elvis record. The old-fashioned album was round and flat and played music like a CD. But it was also larger and solid black. Pefect for a sneak attack.

While Ben jammed, Zoë reared back and threw. The record whizzed through the air like a Frisbee, zooming straight into Axe's guitar.

Twang! Six times! One record broke six strings. Just like that Benjamin Axe's music career was cancelled.

The song on the record? "Jailhouse Rock."

Because the jailhouse was exactly where Benjamin Axe belonged.

Without his guitar, Benjamin Axe was power-less. His hydra crashed into twinkling dust. His headphones shattered. And his mullet mob dried up and blew away in the wind.

He managed to escape himself only by doing something desperate. He cut his hair! After that, he looked like just anyone. He fit into the crowd, as average as could be. He certainly didn't look like a rockstar anymore.

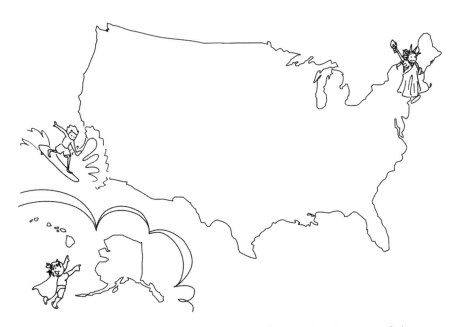

The heroes, on the other hand, had never felt more like rock stars. They had just defeated one of their most powerful foes yet.

"Michigan wasn't enough for us," Andrew bragged. "Today we had to save Ohio. Soon we'll be America's favorite heroes."

Abigail snorted and pointed at her chest. "I've always been the All-American Athlete. What took you so long?"

They both laughed. Michigan, Ohio, America, the world. The heroes always knew they would go wherever danger threatened. They would go wherever and whenever they were needed, from sea to shining sea and beyond.

Today, though, they just went home. Back to Traverse City, Michigan. The Battle of the Bands on the Bay needed to crown a new winner.

Mo and the Hawks. And win they did, by playing loudly, long, and until they were red in the face.

You see, the coolest group in town didn't play rock or hip hop. They didn't even play like a marching band.

Mo and his crew did their own thing. They blew on bagpipes until even the fish in Lake Michigan covered their ears.

Next year things would be different, the heroes told themselves. But they knew it wasn't true. They never had enough time to practice. Superheroes never did. Trouble could strike a chord any day of the year, even at Christmastime in a …

Book #8:
Holiday Hold-up

Visit the Website

realheroesread.com

Meet Authors Charlie & David
Read Sample Chapters
See Fan Artwork
Join the Free Fan Club
Invite Charlie & David to Your School
Lots More!

Also by David Anthony and Charles David

Knightscares

Monsters. Magic. Mystery.

Visit
www.realheroesread.com
to learn more

Real Heroes Read!

#1: Alien Ice Cream
#2: Bowling Over Halloween
#3: Cherry Bomb Squad
#4: Digging For Dinos
#5: Easter Egg Haunt
#6: Fowl Mouthwash
#7: Guitar Rocket Star
#8: Holiday Hold-up

... and more!

Visit
www.realheroesread.com
for the latest news

About the Illustrator
Lys Blakeslee

Lys graduated from Grand Valley State University in Michigan where she earned a degree in Illustration.

She has always loved to read, and devoted much of her childhood to devouring piles of books from the library.

She lives in Wyoming, MI with her wonderful parents, two goofy cats, and one extra-loud parakeet.

Thank you, Lys!